Journey Through the Forbidden Forest

Adapted by Sheri Tan
Illustrated by Antonello Dalena
Colors by Paolo Maddaleni

Ready-to-Read

Simon Spotlight
New York London Toronto Sydney New Delhi

SIMON SPOTLIGHT
An imprint of Simon & Schuster Children's Publishing Division
1230 Avenue of the Americas, New York, New York 10020
This Simon Spotlight edition February 2017
SMURFS™ & © Peyo 2017 Licensed through Lafig Belgium/IMPS. Smurfs: The Lost Village, the Movie © 2017
Columbia Pictures Industries, Inc. and LSC Film Corporation. All Rights Reserved.
For information about special discounts for bulk purchases, please contact Simon & Schuster Special Sales
at 1-866-506-1949 or business@simonandschuster.com.
Manufactured in the United States of America 0117 LAK
10 9 8 7 6 5 4 3 2 1
ISBN 978-1-4814-8058-1 (hc)
ISBN 978-1-4814-8057-4 (pbk)
ISBN 978-1-4814-8059-8 (eBook)

Hi there! My name is Smurfette. Do you want to go on an adventure with Hefty, Clumsy, Brainy, and me? We are looking for a lost village called Smurfy Grove!

Let's go inside the magical
Forbidden Forest!
"One small step for four
small Smurfs," Brainy says.
"One giant leap for Smurfkind."

I have a feeling we are going to see incredible things we've never smurfed before! Are you ready?

When we exit the tunnel, we see
a beautiful sky, trees,
and flowers!
Isn't it so smurfy?

There are all kinds of plants that we don't have in Smurf Village.
Watch out!
Some of them may swallow you up!

There are also Kissing Plants,

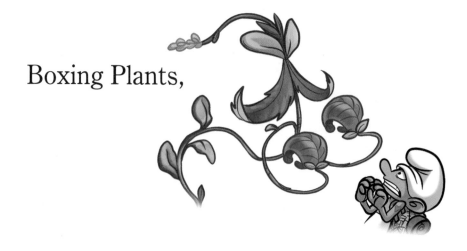

Boxing Plants,

and Eyeball Plants
that watch us as
we walk away!

Look, there are Dragonflies, too!
We stumble into a Dragonfly
nesting ground.
Whatever you do, do not touch
those eggs.
When these Dragonflies get angry,
they breathe fire!

Suddenly, we hear the ground
rumble.
Do you hear that scratching sound?
Stand back!
The Glow-Bunnies are coming!

We get to go for a ride on the backs of the Glow-Bunnies! We even spot rainbow butterflies! Have you ever seen anything more smurfy?

Next, we need to cross an
enchanted river with currents
that float in the air,
so Brainy builds us a raft.
The water is filled with
magical fish and creatures!

The river has lots of rocks.
So we have to be very careful.
Uh-oh!
We are headed toward a
giant waterfall!

Wow! That was a wild ride,
but we are okay.
We relax for a while on a
sandy beach.
That is when we get a surprise.

A group of masked creatures leads
us to a grove filled with trees.
It is called Smurfy Grove,
and the creatures are girl Smurfs!

Back in Smurf Village, we live in mushroom houses, and I am the only girl Smurf around.
Smurfy Grove is totally different. As we enter the village, the girls take off their masks and play trumpets made of flowers!

Houses are made of twigs and leaves,
connected by rope bridges,
and built high up in the trees!
Best of all, there are a total of
one hundred girl Smurfs.
I like it here already!

First, we meet the leader of
the girl Smurfs.
Her name is Smurfwillow.
She makes a grand entrance,
flying in on a spinning flower!

She even throws a party to welcome
us to Smurfy Grove!
Isn't that smurfy?
Then the tour begins!

Do you see the fireflies and caterpillars? In this village, the fireflies are lights and the caterpillars give massages!

There is a math contest,
and Brainy solves an incredibly
long math problem.

There is also a huge gym.
Smurfblossom takes Hefty there,
and he does not want to leave!
"I like to lift stuff," he explains.
"It's my thing."

In Smurf Village, every Smurf
has just one purpose.
Hefty is strong.
Brainy is smart.
Clumsy is clumsy.

In Smurfy Grove, the girl Smurfs
like to do all kinds of things.
We decide to give it a try!
Hefty and Brainy learn to sew.

A girl named Smurfstorm teaches Clumsy how to ride a Dragonfly. He doesn't fall off, and he ends up being a really great Dragonfly rider!

I learn to ride a flowercopter
and play Ping-Pong with my
new Smurf friends!

Things are peaceful right now,
but the girl Smurfs want to keep
their village a secret.
They wear masks
that look like leaves.

They are always ready to
defend Smurfy Grove from
unwanted visitors and are
skilled at archery.
I give archery a try,
and I love it!

In Smurfy Grove, I learned that I can be anything I want to be. Do you want to try something new? Go for it, and be sure to visit again soon!